Ravenspire:

A Sanctuary of Forgotten Souls

By Raji Koshy

Dedication

I express my deepest gratitude to Almighty God, whose unfailing guidance and abundant blessings have sustained me through every day of my life. This is not merely a story—it is a journey, an adventure that began like a distant dream and gradually found its form as a novel.

My heartfelt thanks go to my beloved family for their constant love and unwavering support. I am especially grateful to my parents and grandparents, who once shared stories of these places with me. I have woven those memories together long after they are gone, and I am certain they would have been proud if they were here today.

With love and profound gratitude, I dedicate this book to the alumni committee of St. Joseph's Indian High School, Bangalore; our Director, Rev. Fr. Cyril Menezes SJ; our President and my classmate, Mr. Babu C. Joseph of White Gold; our Vice President, Mr. Vishal Pereira, Director at Creed Cap Asia Advisors; our Secretary, Mr. John Jacob; our Treasurer, Mr. Regy Kurian, Director at Climate Controls; Dr. Arun Kumar; Mr. Ashwin; Mr. Abhishek Shetty; and Mrs. Apeksha Paul—each of whom has taught me invaluable lessons that transformed the way I look at life.

Raji Koshy

Ravenspire

A Sanctuary of Forgotten Souls

- **Raji Koshy**

Detective **Santosh Varma**, once hailed as one of the most intuitive minds in the Bangalore Crime Division, now drifted through his days like a man caught between two realities. He had once been the kind of investigator who could walk into a room and feel the truth hiding behind silence. He could read people like pages—cold killers, crooked ministers, grieving mothers. Nothing escaped his lens. But that man was gone.

Everything had changed the night **Aparna** died.

It was a year ago now, on a rain-slicked mountain road in Wayanad. She had been returning from a solo trip—a short break from city noise and urban decay. Aparna wasn't just his wife. She was the sun that lit the forest in his heart. A botanist by training and a nature photographer by passion, she found serenity in wild places, always chasing beauty with a camera and a sketchbook in her backpack.

That day, she had called him just before her drive back.

"This place is beautiful," she had whispered, wind in her hair, her voice laced with wonder. "But... something feels wrong. I'll be home by nightfall. Can't wait to see your face."

It was the last time he heard her voice.

The call went dead. No final scream, no sound of brakes, just the soft click of a life cut short.

Her SUV was found overturned in a ravine, the body half-buried in red clay and forest moss. No signs of foul play, the police said. A simple accident, they concluded. He knew better.

And yet, he had never questioned the cause. He didn't have the strength. Not back then.

Now, Santosh lived in an apartment that was more mausoleum than home. A third-floor flat in Frazer Town, where the fan blades never stopped spinning and the curtains remained drawn. The windows faced west, but he hadn't seen a sunset in months.

Aparna's belongings remained untouched: her scarves still hung behind the door, her tea mug sat on the kitchen shelf, a wilted cactus by the window clung stubbornly to life. A wooden tripod leaned against the wall like an old soldier on crutches. Her favorite camera, a scratched Canon DSLR with faded stickers, rested on the table as though waiting for her fingers.

He didn't have the heart to box any of it away.

Every night, Santosh sat on the worn armchair by the corner window, a bottle of rum at his feet, and listened to her last voicemail. It had become a ritual. Like a prayer spoken to a god that no longer answered.

"This place is beautiful... but something feels wrong."

He would close his eyes at those words, trying to hear what lay beneath her voice—fear? Curiosity? A warning? Or simply the unease of a traveller sensing something unspoken in the soil beneath her boots?

He often imagined her standing there, in some ancient grove, mist rolling through the undergrowth, camera swinging from her neck, the light falling just right on her face as she smiled and said those words. He would picture her turning, startled, as if she'd heard a voice behind her—and then the image would fade.

Gone was the meticulous detective who once arranged his files by case number and coded them with colour tabs. Now the desk was buried under half-written reports, coffee-stained notepads, and scribbled post-its that made no sense even to him.

He shaved irregularly. His shirt collars grew soft and unkempt. His eyes—once sharp, always watching—now seemed to stare just past the moment, as though trying to find the path back to who he used to be.

His colleagues had stopped checking in. No one blamed him. Tragedy breaks men in different ways. For Santosh, it was as if time had paused at the moment of her death. Every ticking second since was borrowed from a world he no longer believed in.

And yet... there were days when something stirred.

On some mornings, when the birds chirped too brightly or a dream lingered too vividly, he would hear Aparna's voice not as a recording, but alive in the corners of the room. Calling him to wake up. To get up. To follow the thread.

He would shake it off. Pour another drink. Forget again.

But the day a man named **Thomas Abraham** walked into his office, holding a faded photograph and a file full of details asking about a missing girl named **Meera**— the man said he is ready to pay money to find her daughter. On that day, Santosh heard **Aparna's** voice again.

Clearer than before.
Stronger.
"This place is beautiful... but something feels wrong."
And for the first time in a long while, Santosh listened.

It was nearly 7 p.m., and the rusted ceiling fan in Santosh's office spun with a tired groan, echoing the lethargy of the building itself. A half-empty tumbler of cold tea sat on his desk, forgotten amid open case files and scattered cigarette butts. The city's golden hour light bled through the shutters, carving long shadows across the room.

Santosh sat hunched in his chair, lost in the monotony of a police report he wasn't truly reading. His mind drifted, as it often did, toward thoughts of Aparna—toward that voicemail. Toward what it meant.

He didn't hear the door creak open. Only when a soft but firm voice spoke did he lift his head.

"Excuse me... Are you Mr. Varma?"

A man stood in the doorway. Tall, grey-haired, maybe in his late fifties, with eyes that had seen too much grief and not enough sleep. He held a leather satchel clutched to his chest like it might vanish if he let go.

"I'm sorry to barge in like this," the man said quickly. "I've been to five different offices. No one would help. They said you used to take the cases others wouldn't touch."

Santosh studied him silently for a moment before gesturing to the seat across from him.

"Who are you looking for?"

The man sank into the chair and opened his bag. "My name is **Thomas Abraham.** I'm here because of my daughter, **Meera**."

He placed a photograph on the desk.

A young woman smiled back at Santosh. She had intelligent eyes, the kind that hid a mischievous spark, and her hair was tied in a simple bun. She wore no makeup, no pretence. A schoolteacher, Santosh guessed even before Thomas said it.

"She's 28. Teaches primary school. Always wanted to help people. She joined a rural development program last year—government-backed, they said. She was posted to a village in the Western Ghats. A place called..."

He hesitated, almost like he didn't trust the name himself. "...Ravenspire."

Santosh blinked. The name struck him oddly—like something out of a Victorian novel or an old, forgotten fable.

"I've never heard of it," he muttered.

Thomas nodded. "Neither had I. It's not on Google Maps. None of her friends had heard of it either. I only know about it because she wrote it in a letter." He handed Santosh a creased sheet of yellowing paper, worn from too many readings.

Santosh adjusted his glasses and read.

"Appa, the villagers are strange. They smile too much. Say very little. The school is neat, but it's like no one really wants to learn. There's this... fog. It never lifts. And I don't know why, but I feel like I'm being watched all the time."

The letter ended abruptly, as if it had been torn from a longer page.

"I tried contacting the program director," Thomas said, his voice rising slightly. "They claim Meera never reported there. The local police? Useless. Said the village doesn't exist. No record of it, no postal code, nothing. I showed them this letter, but they said it's probably a prank. They refused to file a full missing person's report."

Santosh leaned back, a shadow crossing his face. He'd heard of corruption, of inefficiency—but this was something else. This was... **erasure**.

"I'm not active anymore," Santosh said. His voice was distant, mechanical. "I handle desk cases. Paper trails. Cold files. This isn't my kind of investigation."

Thomas's shoulders slumped. "So they were right. No one cares."

He stood slowly, the photo of Meera still lying on the table. "She's my only daughter," he whispered. "And I know something's wrong. I feel it, every night. My wife passed away five years ago. Meera is all I have. Please."

Santosh didn't respond. He couldn't. The words were too familiar. Too close.

Thomas turned to go. "If you ever change your mind... I'll be in the city for a few more days."

Long after Thomas had left, Santosh sat staring at the letter, then the photo.

He didn't know why he couldn't throw them into a drawer and forget. Maybe it was the look in Thomas's eyes. Maybe it was the letter's final lines—*"...the fog never lifts. And I feel like I'm being watched."* Or maybe it was something deeper.

He poured himself another drink. Then, as he reached for his pen, he accidentally knocked over an old notebook from his shelf—**Aparna's field journal.** It tumbled to the floor, pages fluttering open like wings.

He picked it up, intending to shove it back where it belonged—when something caught his eye.

On the very last page, scribbled in her neat, elegant handwriting:

"Ravenspire – dense forests, eerily silent... I'll come back to sketch this. Reminds me of stories Amma told. A place lost in time."

The glass fell from his hand and shattered on the floor.

Santosh sat frozen. A strange pressure crept into the room, like the air had thickened. His heart pounded in his chest—not just from the mention of the name, but from something else:

A **memory**. A dream. A photograph in Aparna's camera he had never developed. A misty hill. A dark path. A fleeting silhouette.

It wasn't coincidence. Couldn't be.

He pulled open the drawer of his desk, dusted off his old badge, and placed Meera's photo beside it.

Then, he picked up the letter again.
Read it once.
Then a second time.
The last thing he heard that night—before he left the apartment for the first time in weeks—was the familiar echo of Aparna's voice in his mind:

"This place is beautiful... but something feels wrong."

And for the first time in a year, Santosh *felt* again.

He was going to Ravenspire.

The night was deep by the time Santosh powered up his dusty old laptop and began his search.

He typed **"Ravenspire village Western Ghats"** into the search bar.

Nothing.

He tried alternate spellings—*Ravenspyre*, *Ravanspire*, even *Ravanspuram*—but none returned anything relevant. No Wikipedia entry. No tourism forum. No mention in any article, blog, or census record.

Just a line in the void.

He leaned back, chewing on the inside of his cheek, eyes scanning the flickering screen. On a hunch, he pulled up an old contact list. After a few tries, someone picked up—**Radhika Iyer**, a semi-retired cartographer from Mysore, someone Aparna used to consult during her eco-travel articles.

"Radhika," he said, voice low. "Do you remember Aparna ever mentioning a place called Ravenspire?"

There was a pause. Then a slow, wary answer.

"I don't know that name. But I remember Aparna asking me about a forest sector once... a restricted one. She said it had no postal code, no roads leading in. She called it... 'the village behind the veil.'"

"Where?"

"Wayanad side, toward the inner Ghats. She said she saw old

foundations—stone walls, like part of a colonial estate. But every map I checked had it scrubbed clean. Like it never existed."
Santosh thanked her and hung up, heart racing. Aparna had been there. Or near it.

And someone—or something—didn't want it to be found.

Into the Archives

The next day, Santosh visited the **State Land Records Office**, a colonial-era structure near Cubbon Park, where everything smelled of old paper and mothballs. The building held floor-to-ceiling cabinets full of files no one had digitized yet.

A young archivist named **Jayanth**, barely out of college, agreed to help.

"You said the village isn't on modern maps?" Jayanth asked.
"Correct."
"Then we check the **British survey archives**. Some of those villages were abandoned during Partition, or blacked out during post-war border disputes."

They spent hours poring through yellowed sheets, brittle survey maps, and books with red wax seals. At last, under the **1952 Forestry Project Reports**, Santosh found something.

A single-page land survey report:

"District: Wayanad – Forest Code: T-19A
Known Settlement: *Ravenspire*
Population: Estimated 130

Topography: Highland mist belt, evergreen forest perimeter
Status: Restricted zone as of 1971 landslide event – presumed vacated."**

A faint stamp in red ink marked the bottom: **"Project Mnemosyne – Eyes Only – Class B Clearance"**

"What's Project Mnemosyne?" Santosh asked.

Jayanth blinked. "No idea. Sounds Greek. Maybe psychological or military?"

Santosh took a photo of the page, made a copy, and thanked him.

But his gut tightened. This wasn't just a ghost village.

It had been **erased.**

The Journey Begins

The following morning, Santosh packed a small duffel bag—clothes, notebooks, water, torch, camera, a loaded Glock (out of habit more than necessity), and Aparna's field journal.

He studied the faded sketch of Ravenspire's forest ridge she had pencilled in her journal. The trees were gnarled and twisted, the river too narrow to be a main waterway, and a crosshatched path led through them—one she hadn't named. But beneath the sketch, she'd scrawled a single line:

"Follow the dead trees. They don't grow where the fog walks."

Santosh left Bangalore by car just before dawn, heading west. With every mile he crossed, the noise of the city faded, and the air grew heavier, quieter. The road to Wayanad was familiar—he and Aparna had travelled it before, many times, laughing about roadside tea shops and monsoon detours.

But now, the air was different. As if the earth itself remembered something he had forgotten.

By nightfall, he reached a weathered ranger outpost near **Kakkabe**, an unassuming hill station known mostly to trekkers. There, an old ranger named **Rajappa**, grizzled and nearly blind in one eye, watched him closely as he asked for directions to *Sector T-19A*.

"No road leads there anymore," Rajappa said. "Only the *elephant trail*. But it's not used. Not in years."

"Why not?"

"They say fog comes early. Doesn't leave. People lose their way. Some say the trees shift. Some never come back."

Santosh asked for a guide. Rajappa simply shook his head.

"No one goes there. Not unless they're called."

Those words hung in the air, too heavy to ignore.

The next morning, Santosh continued down the road, letting the vehicle move as long as the road allowed, surrendering himself to the rhythm of the journey and the wandering of his thoughts. The pale light of dawn stretched across the asphalt, revealing a path that seemed endless, as though it had no intention of arriving anywhere at all. With every passing mile, memories surfaced uninvited—fragments of faces, unanswered questions, and the quiet weight of truths he had been avoiding.

The road became more than a route; it was a confessional. The hum of the engine blended with the murmur of his mind, each turn urging him forward, each straight stretch daring him to confront what lay within. He did not check the map, nor did he care for destinations. For now, it was enough to keep moving, to let the road decide how far he would go and how deep his thoughts would travel.

The road came to a close almost all of a sudden, as if it had simply decided to end its journey there. What had been a narrow, obedient stretch of asphalt gave way to raw earth and roots, swallowed by a forest that seemed older than memory itself. Towering trees rose on all sides, their thick trunks scarred and weathered, their interlacing branches knitting together to form a dense canopy that filtered the daylight into dim, trembling shafts. Shadows pooled between the trees, heavy and watchful, as though the forest were observing the lone intruder who had dared to enter its domain.

Santosh slowed instinctively, his hands tightening around the steering wheel. A strange unease crept into his chest, the kind that arrives without reason or warning. Before he could fully grasp what lay ahead, the car jolted violently. There was a dull, brutal impact as the front of the vehicle nudged against something solid—an unseen boulder buried beneath layers of fallen leaves, damp soil, and moss that had grown undisturbed for years.

The thud echoed through the car. The tire struck the rock with such force that Santosh was thrown forward, his body slamming toward the steering wheel. Pain flared briefly as his chest and forehead grazed it, and then the world seemed to fold in on itself. Sound drained away. Light dimmed. For a fleeting moment, his thoughts scattered into nothingness, as though someone had switched off his consciousness.

He felt weightless, suspended between waking and darkness. The forest outside blurred into an indistinct haze, and time stretched, thin and uncertain. Then, slowly, sensation began to return—first a dull ache, then the awareness of his own breath, shallow and uneven. The car stood silent, engine stalled, surrounded by towering trees and creeping fog, while Santosh hovered on the edge of consciousness.

Almost immediately, fog began to seep into the clearing, rolling in like a living thing. It thickened with unsettling speed, swallowing the trees, the road, and even the sky above. From inside the car, Santosh could see nothing beyond the windshield—no direction, no familiar shape, only a pale, shifting whiteness pressing in from all sides. The silence felt heavy, broken only by the soft ticking of the cooling engine and his own measured breathing.

A sense of unease settled over him, but so did a strange pull, as though the place itself was urging him to step out. After a moment's hesitation, Santosh opened the door. Cold, damp air rushed in, carrying the earthy scent of wet soil and old leaves. Deciding that staying inside the car offered no answers, he chose to walk, disappearing slowly into the fog that seemed to guard whatever lay ahead.

The trail twisted through undergrowth and fern-draped boulders. At one point, he passed a line of **charred tree stumps**, their bark blackened and dead. No birds chirped here. No monkeys called. Only wind and whispers.

Hours later, the fog arrived.

It didn't roll in gently. It **fell**, like a curtain. Thick. Cold. Sound-muffling. The world narrowed to ten feet in every direction.

He pressed forward, guided only by instinct. And then, just as the forest path began to slope downward—he saw it:

Through the mist, rooftops emerged.
Chimneys. Slanted windows. Cobblestone paths.

Wooden fences. Hanging lanterns.
A town, forgotten by time.

And a wrought-iron sign, covered in rust and ivy:

“Welcome to Ravenspire – A Good Place to Stay Forever”

As Santosh stepped past the wrought-iron gates of **Ravenspire**, the fog lifted—not all at once, but like curtains drawn slowly aside. What lay beyond was not a crumbling, abandoned ghost town.

It was **immaculate**.

Cobbled streets curved gracefully between **quaint English cottages**, each painted in soft pastels and adorned with neatly trimmed hedges. Hanging baskets spilled over with lavender and white petunias. Gas-style lanterns flickered to life even though the sun had barely dipped. Not a scrap of litter. Not a broken window or cracked wall in sight.

And not a single **cell tower**. No buzzing lines, no satellite dishes, not even an electric pole. The place felt... preserved. Like a museum of some lost time, still alive but caged in amber.

As Santosh walked further, he noticed something stranger—**people**.

Not many. Perhaps thirty or forty. All well-dressed in old-fashioned clothes: suspenders, skirts, cardigans, leather shoes. Most seemed to be in their 40s or older. No children played in the lanes. No young voices called. Every head turned as he passed.

They greeted him warmly but cautiously:

"Welcome, sir."
"You made it after all."
"Back with us again?"

He paused at that last one.

"What did you say?"

The man, tall with a salt-and-pepper beard, blinked slowly.

"Just... welcome. That's all."

Santosh nodded, unsettled. There was a delay in their eyes, like actors in a play trying to recall their lines. Smiles stretched too long. No one asked who he was. No one asked what brought him here.

They behaved as if he already **belonged**.

He found the only place that looked like an inn—a broad, two-story colonial house with flower boxes on every window and a hand-carved sign:

"The Haven – Since 1893."

A woman opened the door before he could knock.

Mrs. Lina Devassy, mid-50s, her hair in a precise bun, her eyes too large for her face. She wore a maroon shawl and a knowing smile, as if she'd been waiting for him all day.

"Detective Santosh Varma," she said before he could introduce himself.

"We've prepared your room. You must be tired from the walk."

He froze.

"How do you know my name?"

"Oh, dear. News travels fast. And you're hardly a stranger here, are you?"

Before he could press further, she ushered him in.

The lobby smelled of beeswax and camphor. Old clocks ticked softly. A grandfather clock stood at the far wall, its hands **frozen at 3:17**. A photograph of a much younger Mrs. Devassy stood behind the counter—beside her, a woman who looked unmistakably like **Aparna**. Santosh leaned closer, but the image was faded at the edges, blurred like smoke.

"My wife... did she ever—"

"Many travellers pass through. Some stay. Some forget they were ever here."

She handed him a brass key. Room 4.

"There's hot tea waiting in your room. And no locks, dear. No one here has anything to hide."

That last line rang hollow.

The next morning, after a sleepless night of distant murmurs and dreams of trees with human faces, Santosh walked to the town's only school—a tidy, L-shaped stone building with arched windows and a red tiled roof. Silence floating every where, and a hand-painted board read: **"Ravenspire Central School – Knowledge Is Truth."**

He entered through the side.

The main hallway was lined with framed student artwork, maps of old India, and a fading black-and-white photograph of a past faculty. One face in the photo—just on the edge of the group—was **blurred out completely**.

As he entered the staff room, a soft draft met him. Coffee mugs sat half-drunk on tables. A wall calendar showed **May 1976**.

He found a wooden desk with a brass nameplate:

"Miss Meera Thomas – Class 4B"

Her desk was covered in personal touches. A sketch of a girl reading under a banyan tree. A diary with frangipani petals tucked inside. Her red scarf—the same one from the photo Thomas Abraham had shown him—hung neatly on the back of her chair.

On the chalkboard behind the desk, in neat cursive handwriting:

"Homework: Write about the person who makes you feel safest."

The chalk was fresh. The air in the room... too warm.

He was not alone.

Santosh turned sharply—but the door was empty. No footsteps, no creaking. Just the shifting hush of silence.

He stepped out and asked a passing teacher, a stern-faced woman with rimmed glasses and a pinched voice:

"I'm looking for Meera Thomas. She taught here, yes?"

She blinked.

"I've been here thirty years. Never heard of her."

"Are you sure? Her name is still on the board."

"No one by that name ever worked here."

He showed her the red scarf. She stared at it like it was a dead snake.

"You should leave things where you find them."

Back at the inn, Santosh opened Meera's diary.

The frangipani petals were real—still fragrant. He flipped through pages of lesson plans and doodles, and at the very end, a final scrawled note:

"I see them now. In the mirrors. In the glass.
They smile but they don't blink.
And when they speak... their mouths don't move."

Beneath it, barely legible:

"Tell him I tried. Tell him not to trust—"

The rest was scratched out.

He sat back, heart pounding.
Everything in Ravenspire was too perfect.
Too curated.

As if built for someone.

And now... he feared **that someone was him**.

Detective Santosh Varma stared at the red scarf for what felt like hours. It swayed gently from the back of the wooden chair, disturbed by some unseen breeze in the classroom. The scarf was unmistakably recent—its color vivid, untouched by dust or decay. The board behind the desk still bore chalk markings in neat cursive handwriting:

"History is not what happened, but what we choose to remember."

It was signed beneath in looping script: – *Meera T.*

His throat tightened.

He walked to the headmaster, a thin man with hollow cheeks and rimless spectacles, who had introduced himself simply as "Mr. Solomon." Calm and almost clerical in demeanour, Solomon smiled pleasantly.

"She was never here," he said.

"But that's her handwriting. Her name. Her scarf," Santosh replied, gesturing to the board and the chair.

"Coincidences," Solomon said flatly. "Perhaps you are tired from the journey. Ravenspire can be… disorienting for newcomers."

That night, Santosh walked the streets of Ravenspire, lit by flickering gas lamps and the eerie glow of moonlight filtering through heavy mist. The town was immaculate. Not a speck of dirt, not a single sign of modernity—no wires, no antennas, no cars. The roads were cobbled, not tarred, and the signs were in perfect calligraphy, painted on wood.

Children in neatly pressed uniforms played hopscotch in the square even after sunset. Elderly couples walked slowly with lanterns, whispering softly in an old tongue—Malayalam, but a variant that felt archaic and poetic. Everyone smiled at Santosh.

And everyone knew his name.

"Welcome back, Mr. Varma," the cobbler said.

"Good to see you again, Detective," a little girl with braids whispered.

But he had never set foot in this place.

Had he?

He returned to the inn unsettled. **Mrs. Lina Devassy** awaited him with warm kanji and a side of banana fry. The fire crackled in the hearth. She wore a lace apron over her long skirt and her hair in a bun tied with a white ribbon.

"You'll be more comfortable in Room No. 3," she said. "The one Aparna preferred."

Santosh froze.

"I never mentioned her name."

"Oh," Lina said, with a tilt of her head. "Didn't you?"

Later that night, Santosh explored Room No. 3. The room had a peculiar smell—lavender and something faintly medicinal. Everything felt too neat, as though preserved. The dresser held a mirror so old it was slightly fogged at the edges.

He tapped on the back of the mirror instinctively, remembering a trick from an old smuggling case. The wood echoed hollow.

Removing the mirror revealed a cavity.

Inside, wrapped in linen, was a **small diary bound in black leather**. On the first page was a name in graceful handwriting:

His hands shook as he flipped through the pages.

Drawings of strange trees with leaf patterns he'd never seen. Notes on the silence of birds. Sketches of buildings he'd passed that very day—drawn a year ago. On one page, scrawled hastily in ink smudged by what looked like rain:

"The town forgets. But I remember. This place bends time."

"I met a woman with my mother's eyes. She called me by name before I spoke. Said I'd been here before. I hadn't... had I?"

"If I don't make it out... tell Santosh I was right. Ravenspire is not on any map. Because it exists only when it wants to."

The next day, Santosh pressed harder.

He visited the church, the bakery, the old post office—each establishment welcoming but evasive. Everyone acted as if Meera Thomas had never arrived. At the school, the headmaster had removed her name from the board.

The red scarf was gone.

One girl—a student named **Alya**, barely ten—tugged at his coat as he stood in the village square.

"I saw her," Alya whispered, glancing around nervously. "She used to sing to us after class."

"Where is she now?"

The girl looked up at him with eyes too old for her age. "The forest doesn't give back what it takes."

Before Santosh could ask more, a stern woman, likely her mother, pulled her away.

That evening, he noticed something else: there were no birds in Ravenspire. No dogs. No animals at all. Only the villagers... and the endless fog.

On the third night, a storm rolled in—thunder echoing over the hills. Santosh sat in the inn's reading room, going through Aparna's diary for the hundredth time.

That's when Mrs. Lina appeared.

"I thought you might want this," she said, holding a yellowed photograph. "It was in the old school register."

It was a faded class photo. Rows of children in uniform. A young teacher standing behind them. **Meera Thomas.**

Hair tied, holding a register. The red scarf around her neck. Smiling. Alive.

The photo was dated **April 1959**.

But Meera hadn't even been born then.

The next morning arrived soundlessly.

No birdsong. No rustling leaves. Just fog, as thick as milk, pressing against the windows of the inn. The town seemed muffled, like sound itself had been dampened by something unnatural.

Santosh stood staring at the photograph Mrs. Lina had given him—**Meera Thomas**, clearly in her late twenties, surrounded by children who might have once lived here... decades ago. The photo bore the unmistakable wear of age—creases, faded corners, the sepia tone of a time long passed.

The back of the photograph was handwritten in ink:

"Ravenspire Government School – 12 April, 1959 Faculty: Ms. Meera T."

That date gnawed at his rational mind.

He slipped the photo into his coat pocket and marched to the school again. But this time, he found the gate chained. A padlock hung there, rusted yet secure. No sign of the headmaster. No children playing outside.

The town had turned even quieter, as if **watching him**.

When he turned around, **Alya**, the little girl from before, was waiting by the tree near the square.

She didn't speak. Just stared at him with large, solemn eyes and then pointed toward the **pine forest** on the edge of town.

"She went there," Alya finally said, her voice soft as wind. "That's where she heard the voices. That's where they take people who remember."

Santosh stepped past the stone arch marking the beginning of the pine woods. His boots crunched softly on old pine needles and damp earth. The deeper he went, the colder it became, though the sun still hovered faintly behind the misty canopy.

Every tree looked the same—tall, narrow, suffocating. A trail barely visible wound its way inward, flanked by **eerie carvings** on tree trunks—symbols he didn't recognize, **patterns that repeated in Aparna's old field sketches**.

The forest was silent.

Not quiet—silent. No chirping insects, no rustle of animals. Just an unnatural stillness, as though the world here had paused.

He followed the trail until he saw a **small wooden cabin**, almost invisible through the fog. The door was ajar. Vines crept up its frame. Inside, everything was in place—a table, a chair, a bed. A kettle long rusted. A journal lying open.

Santosh picked it up and read the last entry.

"Day 37 – I think I've been here before. But I don't remember when.
The town changes. Names fade. Faces repeat.
Meera is still singing. But no one else hears her."

He turned to the previous page—there was a sketch of the same classroom he'd seen, with a chilling detail: **Santosh standing in the corner**, drawn from behind.

He hadn't been there when the sketch was made.

Or had he?

He stumbled back, unnerved. That's when he heard it—a faint humming. A melody. A woman's voice.

"Naalum ninne kaanunnathenthinu..."
("Why do I see you every day...")—a Malayalam lullaby his wife used to sing.

He turned toward the sound and walked into the mist. The melody grew louder, closer... and then stopped.

In a clearing, he found **a circle of stones**, covered in moss and carved with the same strange patterns from the forest. In the center stood **an ancient banyan tree**, twisted and blackened by time, its roots exposed like claws.

Beneath it, partially buried in earth, was a satchel. Inside:

- A cracked **Polaroid camera** (Aparna's).
- A mold-stained **field notebook**.
- And a **scarf**—red, tattered, unmistakably Meera's.

But what chilled him to the core was the note pinned inside the satchel:

"If you are reading this, Santosh... you must remember."

"They feed on memory. On time. This place resets. And each time, fewer people return whole."

"We didn't find Ravenspire. It found us."

He sank to his knees, realization dawning in fragments.

Aparna had come here. She had seen something. She had left traces behind. Meera had followed. And now… he was the next in line.

When Santosh emerged from the forest, the sun was lower than it should have been. Hours had passed, maybe days.

But the town was… different.

The streets were dirtier. The shops looked abandoned. The square fountain was dry. And the people—gone.

Only Mrs. Lina stood outside the inn, sweeping the steps.

"Where is everyone?" he demanded.

She looked at him, puzzled.

"Sir… there's been no one here for years."

Santosh walked into the inn. The walls were cracked. Dust coated the shelves. The fire hadn't burned in weeks.

Room No. 3 was locked. When he forced it open, it was empty—stripped bare.

No mirror. No diary. No trace of Aparna.

That night, Santosh sat alone on a bench outside the inn. Fog licked the cobblestones again. Somewhere, a lullaby played faintly on the wind.

"Naalum ninne kaanunnathenthinu…"

The same one.

He realized what was happening—not just to him, but to **everyone who ever found Ravenspire**. The town existed in a **loop**, a temporal whirlpool outside time and space. It **called** certain people—those with unresolved grief, a lingering question, or a sliver of memory linking them to someone already taken.

It offered something. A glimpse of the past. A chance to remember. But at a price.

And then came the voice behind him.

"Detective Santosh Varma?"

He turned.

A young man in a leather jacket stood at the town's entrance. Dusty from travel. Holding a **photograph of his missing brother**.

The same look of disbelief and fear Santosh had worn just days ago.

"I was told you could help me," the man said. "My brother disappeared here. A place called Ravenspire." I have been searching the whole town for few months now.

Santosh felt the fog coil around them both.

He stood up slowly, voice calm, distant, almost mechanical.

"Of course," he said. "Let me see if I can be of any help."

And behind them, the town came alive again.

Santosh did not want to create an environment of suspense around, so he asked him who he was, and he replied his name was Rahul.

Santosh stood at the threshold of sleep for three nights.

In Ravenspire, dreams didn't feel like dreams. They pulsed like memory. Like premonition. One night, he saw Aparna standing beneath the banyan tree, whispering to someone he couldn't see. Another night, Meera's face flickered through static, speaking backwards. Always the same phrase:

"Find the Architect. The town was made."

One morning, Santosh awoke with dried mud on his boots and an old map gripped tightly in his hand. He didn't remember acquiring it, yet it bore his own handwriting.

The map showed Ravenspire not as a village—but as **a construct**, built on concentric rings, almost geometrical in design. Like a **ritual circle**, or a **labyrinth**.

In the centre was marked: **"Sanctum."**

The library in Ravenspire was a neglected building with glassless windows and mold-stained walls. Books filled the shelves—books with no titles, pages filled with scribbled accounts from people long gone. Testimonies. Confessions.

"They ask you to forget. But if you do, they keep you."
– E.C., 1974

"The fog is a membrane. Time slips through its cracks."
– J.A., 1929

"She said we could build a sanctuary for grief. But she lied."
– Rev. Elias Mathen, 1960

Santosh pulled on the cracked floorboards beneath the librarian's desk. Dust rose in a breathless cloud, revealing a **trapdoor**, beneath which spiraled a stone staircase. The air below smelled ancient—like **wet ash, mildew, and memory**.

He descended, torch in hand.

At the bottom was a vaulted chamber: **The Sanctum**.

The walls were engraved with runes and symbols. In the center stood an altar, and behind it... a **statue**.

It depicted a woman cloaked in roots and vines, her hands cupped over her mouth, silencing herself. A plaque read:

"Silva Malini – The Mourner, The Maker."

And next to it, carved deeply into stone:

"In memory we suffer. In forgetting we survive."

: Silva Malini – The Town's Creator

Santosh pieced together fragments from journals, etchings, and visions that grew clearer with every passing day in Ravenspire.

Silva Malini wasn't folklore. She was **real**.

A spiritualist, botanist, and philosopher in the early 1900s, Silva had lost her entire family to plague and war. Her grief consumed her—but she believed grief was not just emotion. She theorized it had **energy**, a psychic weight.

She came to these hills with a group of followers—philosophers, ex-soldiers, exiles—and began to build Ravenspire as a **place to contain pain**. A sanctuary for those who could not move on.

But it wasn't just metaphor.

Through rituals lost to history, **they bound grief to the land itself**, pouring their sorrow into the fog, into the forest, into time.

Over decades, Ravenspire became a **mirror for the broken**, and later, a **trap** for them.

The town would call out—not to the happy, not to the healed—but to those whose pain was unresolved. Who clung to memory like a drowning man to a rope.

Aparna had stumbled into . Meera too. And now... Santosh followed by Rahul now....

In the Sanctum, Santosh found an unfinished ritual scroll—one that could supposedly "unbind" a trapped soul and **sever Ravenspire's grip**.

It required three components:

1. **A personal object of the lost** – He had Aparna's camera and Meera's scarf.
2. **A memory willingly surrendered** – A truth Santosh hadn't faced.
3. **A witness not of the town** – The newcomer, the young man looking for his brother.

Santosh brought the man—**Rahul**—to the Sanctum. He explained everything, and to his surprise, Rahul didn't run.

He stayed.

They placed the items on the altar. As Santosh closed his eyes, he thought of **the voicemail**—Aparna's last words.

"This place is beautiful... but something feels wrong."

He realized something terrible.

Aparna hadn't just died in an accident.

She turned back. She had seen Ravenspire, felt its pull, and tried to leave. The road she died on—**the fog** wasn't natural. The crash... may not have been an accident at all.

He screamed.

Pain tore through him, not just of loss, but of the **lie he'd told himself**—that he had let her go, that he had grieved her.

He hadn't.

He had built **his own Ravenspire** inside.

As the ritual finished, the room trembled. Roots split through stone. The statue of Silva cracked down the middle.

A scream erupted from the earth—not from lips, but from memory itself.

Then silence.

The next morning, Ravenspire was... **gone**.

The square lay in ruins. Cottages collapsed into moss. The school was a shell. The fog had lifted.

Rahul had no memory of the ritual. Only a lingering ache, as though waking from a dream he couldn't name.

Santosh stood at the edge of the pines. The banyan tree had fallen.

He checked his coat pocket.

No photo. No scarf. No diary.

Only a single note, written in Aparna's handwriting:

"You remembered. That's all I wanted."

He looked back once, then turned and walked.

Ravenspire was finished.

Or... perhaps **waiting**, somewhere deeper.

Where grief still lingers. Where memory still haunts. Where the fog still calls.

The inn's common room was dim, lit by a single kerosene lamp that flickered with every draft from the old wooden windows. Mrs. Lina Devassy had retired for the evening, leaving behind a faint scent of cloves and rose oil. The teapot sat on the lace-covered table, steam curling lazily into the air like invisible fingers.

Rahul sat across from Santosh, his eyes scanning the room even as he clasped the warm teacup between his trembling hands. The fire crackled faintly behind them, throwing warped shadows on the faded wallpaper.

"You don't remember how you got here, do you?" Santosh asked.

Rahul shook his head slowly.

"No. Only that I was on my way to a different village. Flood relief work, I think. Took a wrong turn. Or maybe... the road turned me."

Santosh didn't respond immediately. He watched Rahul carefully. The man was fraying at the edges—tired, confused, but not entirely broken. Not yet.

"You said you knew Meera."

Rahul exhaled through his nose, almost a laugh, almost a sigh.

"Not knew. Met. Once. She came to my door a few weeks after I arrived. Still new then. Still herself. She asked questions. About the school, about the children. Said she was hearing voices at night. Seeing lights in the forest."

Santosh leaned in.

"Did she say what kind of voices?"

Rahul looked up slowly.

"Familiar ones. Ones from her past. People she loved. Dead ones."

A chill slipped down Santosh's spine. He thought of **Aparna**, of her final voicemail—the unease in her voice. "This place is beautiful... but something feels wrong."

"Did she say what she found?" Santosh asked.

Rahul shook his head.

"Only that she found a diary. Old, locked. She said it belonged to someone who taught at the school long ago. Someone who disappeared."

That piqued Santosh's attention.

"And the diary?"

Rahul hesitated.

"She hid it. Said she'd show me when she felt safe. But she never came back. A few days later, her room at the teacher's quarters was cleaned out. Like she'd never been there."

Santosh leaned back, heart thudding. He'd seen the **chalkboard**, the **red scarf**, the **nameplate** on her desk—physical proof she existed. But in Ravenspire, nothing stayed anchored. Memories bent. Realities blurred.

"You said we just stay here. What does that mean?"

Rahul stared into his tea.

"This place... it doesn't let you go. Once you've stepped in, it takes something from you. Time, names, even your mind. It feeds on who you were."

He looked up, his eyes suddenly sharp.

"That's why they knew your name. The townspeople. They've seen you before—through others. This place remembers."

Santosh felt something twist in his chest.

"What is Ravenspire?" he asked, voice low.

Rahul swallowed.

"A wound. An echo. A prison, maybe. Or maybe a test. No one's sure. The only people who escape... are the ones who forget they were here. But if you remember—really remember—you never leave."

The clock on the mantle ticked unnaturally loud.

"I remember," Santosh whispered.

The next morning, Santosh returned to the **school** alone. Rahul had disappeared by dawn, leaving only a note on the dresser:

"You'll find it behind the chalkboard. But be careful. Some truths bind tighter than chains."

Santosh pried off the chalkboard, which was set into the wall like a panel. Behind it, buried in the plaster, wrapped in oilcloth, was a **small diary**, its leather cracked with age and a rusted lock still clasped shut.

The initials on the cover made his breath catch: **A.D.**

Anita D'Souza. He had read her name in the archive files—last recorded teacher in Ravenspire before the government blacked out the records in 1957. Missing. Presumed dead.

But here it was. Her diary. Possibly the same one Meera had mentioned to Rahul.

He tucked it into his coat and stepped outside. But the fog was already thick again. As he turned to leave the schoolyard, a **child's voice** called from the mist:

"Mister Santosh... are you going to save her?"

He turned. No one was there.

Just the red scarf... caught in the branches of a tree.

Back in his room at the inn, Santosh locked the door behind him and sat at the edge of the bed, the worn diary in his lap. The lock looked delicate, but aged—fragile enough to pry open with a knife. He worked slowly, carefully.

With a soft snap, the lock gave way.

The scent of old paper, ink, and mould drifted up. The pages were brittle, handwritten in elegant cursive. On the inside cover, a name:

Anita D'Souza, Ravenspire Primary School, 1956.

Santosh turned the first few pages. What started as an innocent teacher's journal quickly grew darker with every entry. She had come to Ravenspire as part of an education outreach program—just like Meera.

At first, her entries were full of admiration for the untouched natural beauty. The kind children. The polite villagers. But by the third week, her tone shifted.

July 3, 1956
Something is wrong with the children. They speak of things I've never taught. Words in dialects that don't belong here. One child said he saw me "long ago." I asked what he meant. He only smiled.

July 7, 1956
No birds. No animals. Not even insects. Ravenspire is silent, too silent. Lina (the same woman? Santosh wondered) told me the forest doesn't want to be disturbed. What does that mean?

July 12, 1956
The villagers avoid mirrors. I asked why. One man said, "You don't want to see what looks back." I tried to laugh it off—but when I looked into the inn's mirror this morning, I saw a girl standing behind me. She had my face. But younger. And afraid.

Santosh rubbed his forehead. This wasn't just a record. It was a **warning**. He flipped further.

July 18, 1956
I am beginning to forget things. My own birthday. My mother's face. The name of my dog. I tried writing them down, but the ink fades. The villagers call it "The Unravelling."
Lina says I'm resisting the town, and that resistance has a price.
I must hold on.
I must remember.
I must remember.
I must remember.

The next few pages were smeared, words overwritten again and again.

Then—abrupt clarity.

July 22, 1956
I found the truth. This place is a **veil**—a fold in time and memory. A relic from a time when rituals still bound land and soul. The villagers aren't evil. They are trapped. Ravenspire isn't alive... it's *conscious*. And it feeds on **remembrance**.

The people who vanish don't die.
They are... rewritten.
The only way to escape is through **The Memory Rite**—a ritual that seals your memories behind a mask of forgetfulness. Once forgotten, Ravenspire lets you go.

But I won't leave.
Not yet.
Not until I find out what happened to the others.
The ones who came before me.
Including the girl in the woods.
The one who keeps whispering...
"Don't trust him."

Santosh's breath caught.

The same phrase Meera wrote in her last letter.

A sudden knock on the door snapped him out of his trance.

He froze. The diary slipped from his lap.

The knock came again—firm, rhythmic.

Santosh opened it slowly.

It was Mrs. Lina.

"Mr. Varma," she smiled gently. "You've been reading."

Santosh narrowed his eyes.

"What is this place?"

She tilted her head.

"A haven. A curse. A mirror. It becomes what you bring with you."

"What happened to Anita? And Meera?"

Her smile faded for the first time.

"They stayed too long. And remembered too much."

Then she added, softly, almost kindly:

"You still have a chance, Santosh. The forest remembers Aparna. Her grief. Her longing. She opened a path for you."

He was stunned.

"Aparna was here?"

Lina nodded.

"Not long before her accident. She came searching for rare orchids. But found something else. A memory not hers... but one she couldn't forget."

"And you let her leave?"

Lina's voice was almost a whisper now.

"She chose to remember. And Ravenspire doesn't forgive memory."

Santosh felt the floor tilt beneath him. His head spun. The fog outside pressed against the windowpanes like a living thing. Somewhere in the hallway, a child was humming an old lullaby in a language he couldn't understand... but felt like he once knew.

He staggered back into the room, picked up the diary.

There—tucked in the back cover—was a sketch.

Of a **stone altar** in the middle of a forest clearing. And next to it: **Aparna**, drawn in Anita's hand, unmistakably.

And below it:

"If you must leave, find the altar before the moon wanes. But remember... some doors require memory to close."

The sketch of the stone altar burned in Santosh's mind. The forest, it seemed, waited.

He left the inn before dawn. The villagers watched silently from their porches, eyes dull like fading photographs. None spoke. None tried to stop him.

He passed the rusted school gate where Meera's name had once hung on the board. Past the withered trees behind the chapel, where Anita's diary said the veil thinned.

The fog parted like curtains as he walked, revealing an overgrown path only visible when not looking directly at it. The forest was suffocatingly silent, as if even nature feared what lay deeper within.

Hours passed.

Or was it minutes?

Time frayed.

There it was.

Half-buried in roots and moss, the **stone altar** stood like a forgotten monument from another age. Intricate carvings covered its surface—snakes eating their tails, eyes without pupils, a sun eclipsed.

In the centre: a weathered mask carved from bone-white wood.

Santosh reached out and touched it.

A violent **flash of memory** hit him—**not his own**.

A woman screaming in an unknown tongue.
Meera, bound and terrified.
Anita's voice whispering, "Don't let them rewrite her."

And then—**Aparna**.

She stood before the altar, alive, weeping.

"I remember now," she whispered in the vision. "And I can't go back."

Santosh fell to his knees. The weight of it all—memory, grief, guilt—crushed him.

Behind him, footsteps.

He turned.

Rahul emerged from the mist. The young man he'd met earlier—calm, polite, too polite. But now, something about his eyes had changed. Too still. Too knowing.

"You shouldn't be here," Rahul said.

"I came for Meera," Santosh replied.

Rahul looked almost sympathetic.

"She's part of Ravenspire now. Like the others. Like me."

Santosh stared at him.

"Who are you?"

Rahul tilted his head.

"Once, I was a boy from Delhi. I got lost on a school trip. I don't remember my parents' faces anymore. Ravenspire gave me a new story. I just stopped fighting."

He gestured to the mask.

"That's your way out. But if you put it on... you forget. Everything. Aparna, Meera, even your own name. Ravenspire will let you go, but you'll never know who you were. Or why you came."

"And if I don't?"

"Then you stay. And slowly, you forget anyway."

The trees around them groaned. Time was unraveling.

Santosh looked at the mask. It seemed to pulse faintly in his hand, like it was alive.

From the shadows, a voice echoed—

Meera's voice.

"Don't forget me..."

The forest around him dissolved into **shards of moments**:

- Aparna smiling, camera in hand.
- A red scarf caught in barbed wire.
- A chalkboard covered in strange symbols.

- Anita writes furiously by candlelight.
- A little boy looking in a mirror and screaming.

Then—**nothing**.

Blackness.

When Santosh came to, he was **standing at the altar**.

The mask was gone.

In his pocket, Anita's diary had turned to dust.

And across from him, standing silently, was **Meera**.

She looked dazed, her eyes unfocused.

"Santosh...?" she whispered.

He stepped forward, relieved—until he saw **his reflection** in her eyes.

His face was younger. Confused. And he was wearing **the mask**.

He staggered back.

Rahul stood beside him now.

"You put it on."

"No... I didn't—"

"You did. And Ravenspire let you remember long enough... to realize you've become part of it."

"But I found her. Meera—"

"You did. But she's *your echo now*. The town reshaped her. Like it did Anita. Like it did Aparna. They never truly leave."

Santosh looked around.

The forest was gone.

Only mist.

And faint outlines of **buildings**, **people**, **memories**—looping endlessly.

The villagers... they weren't villagers.
They were **stories**, played over and over again.

Trapped souls, reliving fragments of who they once were.

And now... **so was he**.

Santosh felt... light.

Not the kind of light that follows relief or joy—but something else. Weightless. As if gravity itself had forgotten him. His limbs floated, his thoughts dissolved. The woods around him were no longer threatening; in fact, they looked serene, almost ethereal.

The heavy, choking fog that once pressed against his chest now felt like a warm breeze brushing through him. His mind, so long wrapped in doubt and dread, had gone still. Still and... **silent**.

"I must have fainted," he told himself, though no memory preceded this calm.

He blinked.

Now he was lying gently on the moss-carpeted forest floor. He didn't remember falling. But he wasn't alarmed. In fact, he smiled faintly.

"This... this is peace."

He rose. His body moved with uncanny ease, as though air passed through him. The twigs beneath his feet didn't crack. The leaves didn't rustle. It was like walking through a dream.

Then he saw it.

Through the lattice of trees and hanging mist, his **car** stood half-visible—crumpled and silent beneath a towering banyan. The front was crushed inward, metal curled like paper, steam hissing from under the broken hood. Glass sparkled across the forest floor like pieces of a shattered mirror.

Santosh frowned. A quiet unease began to creep into his chest.

"What happened?"

His pace quickened—he still didn't feel the ground.

No thud. No crunch. Just a gliding, almost **glitching** movement toward the wreckage.

The closer he came, the stronger the dread.

And then he saw it.

The driver-side door hung open, creaking slowly with the breeze.

Inside, slumped grotesquely over the steering wheel, was a man—his face bloodied and half-hidden by shattered glass. The airbag had exploded. His chest was crushed. One arm dangled out of the window, the watch on his wrist still ticking faintly.

Santosh stared.

He felt the blood drain from his soul.

"No... no..."

It was **him**.

His own face, twisted and frozen in a moment of impact. His own hands, pale and broken. His own coat. His own scent lingering in the air.

A dry wind howled through the forest.

“This isn’t real,” he muttered. “This can’t be...”

But something deeper inside him—**something ancient and knowing**—whispered:

You never left the woods.

He staggered back, but his legs didn’t obey like before. He floated, yes—but now it felt **wrong**. His fingers passed through the door handle. His breath didn’t fog the glass. The wind moved through him.

Around him, the woods began to shift.

The trees were bending inward now. Faces emerged in the bark—silent, watching. Eyes without irises. Mouths locked in grimaces.

Then, voices.

Whispers. At first unintelligible, then clearer.

“He knows...”
“He saw himself...”
“Too late...”
“Another memory, another ghost...”

From the shadows, shapes moved—**people**, maybe. Villagers. Children. A woman in a red scarf. Aparna. Meera. Rahul. All with **empty eyes**, like paper dolls animated by forgotten memories.

They circled him.

Santosh screamed—only to realize there was **no sound**. His voice was **gone**. His mouth moved, but nothing came out.

He looked at his hands—**transparent**. The outlines of trees could be seen through his skin.

"No... I'm not dead... I'm not..."

But the truth pressed in like cold fingers on his spine.

Ravenspire hadn't been a town. It had been a **trap**.

Not of brick or stone, but of **memory** and **unfinished stories**. A place that preyed on the lost, the grieving, the curious. Those offered answers, only to **feed on those who asked**.

And now Santosh had become one of them.

The floating sensation... was his **soul** being absorbed. The peace he felt... was **submission**. The whispers... were the **voices of others** who'd tried to resist.

He turned toward the villagers forming a circle.

Mrs. Lina was among them. Smiling, like always.

"Welcome home, Mr. Varma," she whispered. "You found what you were looking for. Now let us carry the weight of your story."

And then they came closer. Not walking—but **gliding**, like puppets.

Santosh tried to run, but running no longer meant anything. His legs moved without distance, his breath without urgency. Every direction dissolved the moment he chose it. The forest folded into itself, paths bending back like memories misremembered, trees shifting just enough to erase intention.

The ground softened beneath him, swallowing his footprints as though he had never existed, as though the earth itself refused to acknowledge his passing.

Fog rose—not drifting, but blooming—thick and deliberate. It wrapped around him in slow, patient spirals, until the car vanished, then the altar, then the faces he had once known, loved, feared. Even the idea of a face became difficult to hold. The fog was not empty; it was full—of whispers, of echoes, of moments that no longer belonged to time.

Only one sound remained. His heartbeat.

At first it thundered in his ears, frantic and defiant, clinging to the lie of life. Then it began to slow. Each beat stretched farther apart, like footsteps fading down a long corridor. The sound deepened, changed, lost its urgency. It was no longer *his* heartbeat. It merged with something larger—older—a steady pulse that seemed to rise from the soil itself, from the roots beneath the town, from the walls that remembered every scream and every prayer ever uttered there.

He understood then what it meant to be dead.

Not silence. Not darkness. But dilution.

His thoughts thinned, spreading out like ink in water. Words lost their edges. Emotions arrived without names. Fear lingered longest, not sharp but dull, like a bruise that never healed. He tried to hold onto himself—to his name, his face, the weight of his body—but these things slipped through him, intangible, ungraspable.

The car remained there in the woods, seasons passing unnoticed. Rust bloomed along its edges like a slow infection.

Leaves gathered, then buried it. Rain seeped in. Time did what time always does—patient, merciless work.

Inside, Santosh's body sat motionless.

Flesh softened. Bone emerged. What had once been him became matter again, decomposing, anonymous, forgotten by the world above. No marker. No farewell. Just a shape surrendering to the forest.

But death did not end him. It scattered him.

His soul did not rise or fall; it lingered. It pressed itself thin against the boundaries of the place, tethered by unfinished fear and unanswered questions. He could not leave, because leaving required knowing *where* to go. He could not rest, because rest required knowing *who* he was.

And at times—on cold mornings when the fog lay heavy and the forest seemed to hold its breath—something strange would occur.

If you walked by, you might hear it.

A faint sound.

Not a scream. Not a cry.

A tapping. From inside the car.

Softly. Desperately. Not asking to be saved.

Not asking to be found.

Just trying—again and again—to remember his name.

Other Fictions by the Author

1. 6 Scary Stories. - Short Stories
2. The Staircase to Nowhere
3. Don’t Scream in the Dark
4. Riddle from the Grave
5. The Encounters
6. Underground.
7. The Midnight Passenger
8. They still live among us

The author would be delighted to hear your thoughts on this book. To join the reader community on WhatsApp, simply send a message saying “Book reader” to +91 9900570221.

Disclaimer

All characters, events, and entities featured in this book are entirely fictional. Any resemblance to actual persons, living or dead, or to real-life events, is purely coincidental and unintentional.

First Edition – January 2026
ISBN Number: 978-93-5626-864-7

eBook ISBN No: 978-93-5636-929-0

ISBN 978-93-5626-864-7 US$3.99

Cover Design by: **Raji Koshy**
Printed in INDIA

For permissions or inquiries, contact:

+91 9900570221
rajikoshy@gmail.com

www.ingramcontent.com/pod-product-compliance
Lightning Source LLC
Chambersburg PA
CBHW062202160726
48282CB00027B/968

* 9 7 8 9 3 5 6 2 6 8 6 4 7 *